It's Your First Kiss,

Charlie Brown
Charles M. Schulz

Random House • New York

Library of Congress Cataloging in Publication Data

Schulz, Charles M. It's Your First Kiss, Charlie Brown. SUMMARY: Charlie Brown panics when selected to escort the
homecoming queen to the big post-football game dance. [1. School stories] I. Title. PZ7.S38877Iu [E] 78-7460
ISBN: 0-394-83955-2   ISBN: 0-394-93955-7 lib. bdg.

Manufactured in the United States of America

1 2 3 4 5 6 7 8 9 0

I don't understand this escort business, Linus. What does an escort do?

It's simple, Charlie Brown. We escort the queen and her attendants to the dance after the football game.

Good grief!

Glub . . . gasp! Linus, that girl . . . it's . . .

You mean Heather?

Heather! Gasp! It's . . . it's . . . the
little red-haired girl!

She's the Homecoming Queen. And you, Charlie Brown, are supposed to escort her to the ball. According to tradition, you escort Heather to the center of the ballroom. Then, before the first dance begins, you have to give her a kiss!

All right, team, let's pay attention. We're not gonna play
around with those guys out there today.

Our basic play will be me,
Peppermint Patty, smashing
straight ahead and grinding out
the yards.

You guys up front set them back
on their heels. I'll do the rest!

Are there any questions?

Yes, are we the zeros or the *x*'s?

I mean, are we the zeros or the *x*'s?

What do you mean, are we the zeros or the *x*'s?

That's a good question. I'm glad to see you guys are thinking.

Now let's go out there and get to work!

YEAH!

LET'S GET 'EM!

FIGHT!

FIGHT!

Are we the zeros or the x's?

Let's get the game started, kicker.

What happened?
They must have blocked it.

You missed the ball, Charlie Brown.
They ran right over you.

I'd better practice up on place kicks.

Hut one! Hut two! Hut three!

Linus, are you sure that I'm supposed to be Heather's escort?

Sure, Charlie Brown.

At the dance you're supposed to walk up to the queen. She'll take your arm. You'll escort her to the dance floor. And then before the dance starts, you'll give her a kiss on the cheek. It's a tradition.

Oh, good grief, Charlie Brown!

Okay, Chuck, it's time for the extra point. I'll give you a chance to be a hero. Boot one between the old uprights!

Chuck, you really goofed up
on that play!

Too bad, Charlie Brown. That
leaves them ahead. Now you have
to go back for the kickoff.

Hold it there,
Charlie Brown.

We don't need a kicking
tee. *I'll* hold the ball.

Are you CRAZY?
You'll pull it away,
and I'll land flat
on my back again!

This is a very important game,
Charlie Brown. Do you think I'd
pull the ball away in an important
game like this?

Well, okay. I guess it's true. This is too important a game. She wouldn't dare pull that ball away.

What happened?
I feel woozy.

Maybe you have
hyponatremia. All
you need is a little
water and a little
salt.

Oh, brother!

To answer your question, Franklin, about the *x*'s and the zeros, I think we found out who our zero is!

Okay, gang, they've got us by only two touchdowns. I know we can make that up and more. The only weakness I can see is our kicking game. Luckily, next half they kick off to us. Now let's get out there and ram it down their throats!

Linus, I've made a fool of myself. How can I face that little red-haired girl?

Look at it this way, Charlie Brown. It's better to get bad press than no press at all.

I doubt that, Linus. Look at her up there. I'm going to be her escort, and she doesn't even know I exist.

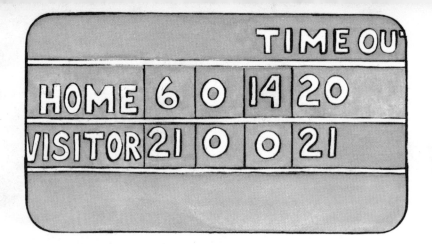

Well, we can't push them back. We'll have to go for a field goal. We're on the five-yard line. *Nobody* could miss such an easy kick—not even you know who!

Okay, Charlie Brown, the score is twenty-one to twenty. We need three points to go ahead. You can do it. You can be the hero of the game.

CHUCK! You can't do anything right!

They beat us
by one point.

Hey, Chuck, what are you doing here? After you just lost today's game, this is the last place we thought you'd be.

But I'm the escort for the queen tonight.

HA HA HA

What a laugh! Who'd want to be your date after today's game!

Gee, Charlie Brown, you look terrible. You'd better cheer up. You've got to escort the queen, you know.

Don't you realize what's happening? I'm going to escort the little red-haired girl! And . . . and kiss her!

She's my dream girl!

Next morning....

PROGRAM

HOME COMING
FOOTBALL
GAME
—BALL—

Hi, Charlie Brown. That game yesterday was a heartbreaker.

There was a game?

Golly, one point! They won by one point! Too bad you missed that field goal, Charlie Brown.

But at least the dance turned out to be a real success, didn't it? You surprised everyone when you gave Heather that long, passionate kiss.

Kiss?

Boy, you really swept her off her feet when the dance started. You were fantastic, Charlie Brown! You were the life of the party. You lost the football game, but you sure took honors at the dance!

Did I do all that? What good is it to do anything if you can't remember what you did?

Well, at least it was your first kiss, Charlie Brown.